This edition published by Parragon Books Ltd in 2016 and distributed by

Parragon Inc.
440 Park Avenue South, 13th Floor
New York, NY 10016
www.parragon.com

ISBN 978-1-4748-6592-0

Printed in China

Goodnight
Little One

PaRragon

Bath • New York • Cologne • Melbourne • Delhi
Hong Kong • Shenzhen • Singapore

Little donkey on the hill,
Standing there so very still.

Making faces at the skies,

Little donkey
close *your* eyes.

Little monkey in the tree,
Swinging there so merrily.
Throwing coconuts at the skies,

Little monkey
close *your* eyes.

Silly sheep that slowly crop,
Night has come and you must stop.

Chewing grass beneath the skies,
Silly sheep now close *your* eyes.

Little pig that squeals about,
Make no noises with your snout.

No more squealing to the skies,

Little pig now
close *your* eyes.

Wild young birds that sweetly sing,
Curve your heads beneath your wing.
Dark night covers all the skies,
Wild young birds now close *your* eyes.

Old black cat down in the barn,
Keeping five small kittens warm.
Let the wind blow in the skies,

Dear old black cat
close *your* eyes.

Little child all tucked in bed,
Looking such a sleepy head.
Stars are quiet in the skies,

Little child now
close *your* eyes.